MAMA LLAMA'S PAJAMAS

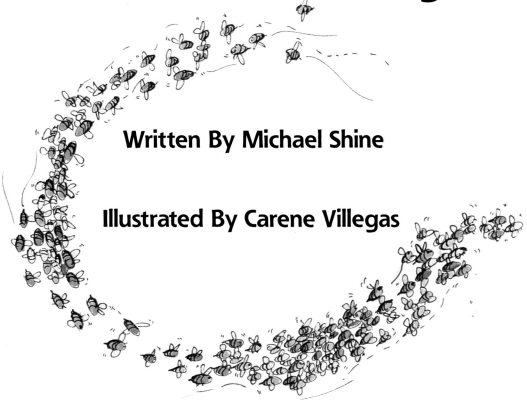

Written By Michael Shine

Illustrated By Carene Villegas

Romar Books Ltd.
Seattle Washington

Published by Romar Books Ltd.
18002 15th Avenue NE, Suite B
Seattle, Washington 98155-3838

Printed and bound in Hong Kong

Typesetting and layout by ODAAT Business Publishing Services

ISBN 0-945265-32-8

To all people young and old
who need to understand how
important they are.

Bruce Moose gave a big sigh, "I have horns, but I don't know why."

Meanwhile, Mama Llama had washed her pajamas and hung them up to dry.

Then off she ran through the meadow lands to swim in the lake nearby.

Soon a breeze blew through the trees and whisked her pajamas away — WHOOSH! Off they flew like a bright white kite —

Until PLOP! — they landed on Ollie Owl! Poor Ollie! Everything became darker than night.

"WHO! WHO!" cried Ollie, as he flew through the trees. "WHO turned out the lights, if you please?"

Bruce Moose shook in his boots as Ollie Owl flew by.

"Oh my gosh, it's a **ghost**!" he cried, and he quickly ran to hide.

Finally Ollie crashed — KA-POW — into a tree.

And wouldn't you know, he landed below, on a hive of busy bees!

The bees stung Ollie, and, by golly, Ollie shouted, "OW!"

Around and around he danced and pranced like a funny feathered clown!

Bruce Moose heard Ollie shout, and ran to help him out. Mama Llama heard it too, and came to see what she could do.

On Ollie flew, not aware he was heading straight for Claire Bear's lair. Claire Bear gave such a terrible growl, she blew the pajamas right off Ollie Owl!

The pajamas landed on the swarm of bees
who buzzed the pajamas through the trees —

past Tickle Meadows,

over Ice Cream Mountain,

and across Hiccup Creek.

They all chased after the crazy pajamas until their legs were weak.

A sudden wind blew the pajamas loose, from the swarm of bees onto the horns of Bruce Moose!

"My, oh my," laughed Mama Llama,
"what a fine clothesline for my pajamas!"

"How divine!" agreed Claire Bear. "I'd love to dry my laundry there!"

Bruce Moose admitted it might be fun. "When I take a nap, I'll have shade from the sun!"

Now when Bruce rests near the pasture of the Llamas, guess what you will see on his horns!

Of course! Mama Llama's pajamas!